A WISHING SHELF BOOK REVIEW

18th September, 2019

TITLE: Daddy Long Legs
AUTHOR: Jean Webster
Abridged by Fiza Pathan and Michaelangelo Zane and Illustrated by Farzana Cooper
Star Rating: 4

CATCHY QUOTE

'A well-written and very accessible abridgment of the classic Daddy Long Legs. Perfect for introducing this text to 7 to 12 year olds.' The Wishing Shelf

REVIEW

I'm not going to comment too much on the story only to say it was originally written by Jean Webster and is very much a coming-of-age tale of a girl's life at college and the letters she sends to her benefactor, a person she has never met. It is very much a joyful story, as Judy tells the 'tall, thin man' – which is why she calls him Daddy Long Legs – all about her fun, exciting life.

Although I am a big fan of the book, I do think the message is a little dated. I think the author honestly thinks that an orphan can be put in a new 'rich' environment and all his/her problems will simply fly away. Sadly, it's not like that; the mental scars suffered by children can stay with them for a long time, if not forever. But, let's not dwell on that. There's so much 'goodness' in this story, I think children today will get a lot from it. And I'm delighted that authors like Fiza Pathan and Michaelangelo Zane are producing abridgments of these classics.

All in all, this is a very good attempt. The authors work hard to keep the original message and much of the plot, whilst simplifying a text originally published in 1912. If you didn't know, the whole text is in the form of letters. Yes, letters! I wonder if, today, children even know what a 'proper' letter is. But it will do them good to show them!

I could see the abridgment working very well as a class reader in a primary school. The pacing is excellent and this abridgment has left in all the good stuff, so there's much for children to discuss. Also, there are a number of black and white drawings which do add to the text and, I think, will help children to stay focused on the story.

I would happily recommend this book to any school library or parent looking to introduce a child to the classic text without overwhelming them with the flowery text of the original.

A 'Wishing Shelf' Book Review

www.thewsa.co.uk

Daddy-Long-Legs

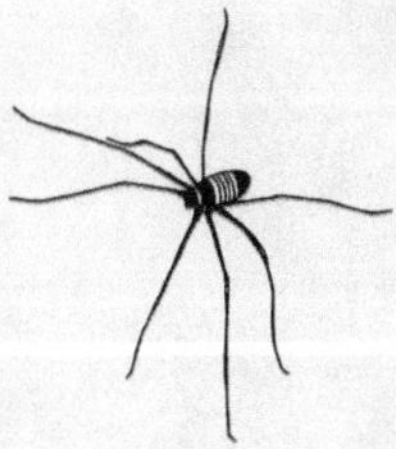

Jean Webster

Daddy-Long-Legs

Jean Webster

Abridged by Fiza Pathan and Michaelangelo Zane
Illustrated by Farzana Cooper

Fiza Pathan Publishing OPC Private Limited

Mumbai, INDIA

Rare Classics

Imprint. Freedom With Pluralism®
Fiza Pathan Publishing OPC Private Limited
Symbol Apts., Flat No 2, Tertullian Rd, Off Dr. Peter Dias Road,
Bandra West, Mumbai 400050, INDIA
Email. fizapathan@fizapathanpublishing.com
Website. https://fizapathanpublishing.us/

Illustrated by Farzana Cooper.
Cover art and design. Farzana Cooper and LLPix Cover Art & Design
This book contains 16 original black and white illustrations and a color cover art, commissioned by author Fiza Pathan and executed by Farzana Cooper. All rights reserved.

Book Layout © 2017 BookDesignTemplates.com

Daddy-Long-Legs/ Webster, Jean. Abridged by Pathan, Fiza and Zane, Michaelangelo- 1st ed.

ISBN 978-81-938201-8-6 Hardback
ISBN 978-81-938201-9-3 Paperback

Daddy-Long-Legs

Blue Wednesday

The first Wednesday of every month at the John Grier Home for the Orphans was always an awful day, a day the children awaited with dread. The floors had to be spotless, every chair dustless, and every bed without a wrinkle. Ninety-seven squirming little orphans had to be scrubbed and combed and buttoned into freshly starched overalls. All ninety-seven of them were reminded of their manners and told to say, "Yes, sir" or "No, sir" whenever a trustee spoke.

The trustees of the John Grier Home inspected the orphanage on the first Wednesday of every month. It was a distressing time for all, but poor Jerusha Abbott, being the oldest orphan, bore the brunt of it.

Jerusha had been on her feet since five that morning, doing everybody's bidding while being scolded and hurried by the most dutiful Mrs. Lippett. That evening, after leaving the kitchen, she went to room seven where she had the duty of looking after eleven toddlers between the ages of four and seven. She straightened their rumpled clothes and sent them in an orderly line to the dining room to eat their meager dinner of bread, milk, and prune pudding.

The day had ended quite successfully as far as Jerusha was concerned. The trustees and the visiting committee had made their rounds. They read their reports, drank their tea, and now they hurried home to their cheerful firesides to forget the burdensome little charges for another month. Jerusha leaned forward, watching with curiosity the stream of carriages and automobiles that rolled out of the asylum gates.

"Jerusha Abbott, you are wanted in the office," came a cry from one of the choirboys, as he passed room seven where Jerusha was sitting and staring out of the window.

Jerusha went without comment, but with her brow furrowed into two parallel lines. *What could have gone wrong?* she wondered. *Were the sandwiches not thin enough? Did some shells get in the nut cakes? Had one of her angelic room seven babies sassed a trustee?*

As Jerusha arrived downstairs, she noticed the corridor was dimly lit. A man came out of Mrs. Lippett's office. She couldn't make out his face or anything specific about him, except that he was a gentleman of unusually tall height. As he opened the door of the asylum and proceeded to his automobile, his shadow was cast upon the wall. To Jerusha it resembled a large spider—a huge and wavering daddy longlegs.

Jerusha's anxious frown quickly gave way to laughter. She advanced to the office quite cheered by the tiny episode and presented a smiling face to Mrs. Lippett, the strict orphanage matron. To her surprise, the matron was also smiling.

"Sit down, Jerusha. I have something to say to you."

Jerusha dropped into the nearest chair and waited with a touch of breathlessness. An automobile flashed passed the window. Mrs. Lippett glanced after it.

"Did you notice the gentleman who just left?"

"I saw his back," Jerusha replied.

"He is one of our richest trustees and has given a large sum of money for the asylum's support. I cannot mention who he is or what his name is, as he expressly stipulated that he must remain unknown."

To Jerusha the man's shadow resembled a large spider

Jerusha's eyes widened. She was not accustomed to being summoned to the office to discuss the eccentricities of the trustees with Mrs. Lippett.

Mrs. Lippett told her how this particular trustee took an interest in promoting the education of orphaned boys. She even mentioned the names of particular boys put under the care of the trustee, whose kindness was repaid with the boys' hard work and success.

"I have never been able to interest him in any of the girls in the institution in even the slightest degree, no matter how deserving," said Mrs. Lippett severely. "He does not care for girls."

"No ma'am," Jerusha murmured, since she felt that some reply was expected at this point.

"However," continued Mrs. Lippett, "today at the meeting, the question of your future was brought up."

There was a moment of silence after which Mrs. Lippett said, "Usually children are not kept after a certain point here at the asylum, but in your case, Jerusha, because you've excelled in your studies, we managed to send you to high school. You have finished high school now, and we were going to let you go, until this trustee discovered that your work in English has been brilliant."

Mrs. Lippett mentioned an essay Jerusha had written titled "Blue Wednesday," a humorous composition that ridiculed the monthly Wednesday rituals.

"It seemed to me, Jerusha, that in that essay, you showed little gratitude for all that our institution has done for you. However, to your luck, this trustee has an unusual sense of humor. And, on the basis of that ridiculous composition, he has offered to send you to college."

"To college!" Jerusha's eyes grew big with delight.

Mrs. Lippett said that the gentleman thought she should become a writer. He would send her to college and pay for both board and tuition with his own money. She would never know who the trustee was, and any necessary communication—meaning only matters of urgency—would pass through the trustee's private secretary. The gentleman, being eccentric, had asked for a very peculiar mode of thanks to come from Jerusha. She would, on a monthly basis, write a letter of acknowledgment to the gentleman, reporting the progress in her studies and the details of her daily life.

"These letters will be addressed to Mr. John Smith," said Mrs. Lippett, "and will be sent in care of his secretary. The trustee's name is not John Smith, but he will never be anything but John Smith to you."

Jerusha was also informed that Mr. John Smith, in his turn, would never answer her letters.

"You must remember that you are writing to a trustee of the John Grier Home," were Mrs. Lippett final words, and Jerusha took her leave.

Jerusha Abbott

The Letters of Miss Jerusha Abbott to Mr. Daddy-Long-Legs Smith.

215 Fergussen Hall,
September 24

Dear Kind-Trustee-Who-Sends-Orphans-to-College,

Here I am! I traveled yesterday for four hours in a train. It's a funny sensation, isn't it? I never rode in one before.

College is the biggest, most bewildering place; I get lost whenever I leave my room. I will write you a description later. I will also tell you about my lessons. Classes have not yet begun, but I wanted to write a letter first just to get acquainted.

It seems queer to be writing letters to somebody I don't know. It seems odd for me to be writing letters at all—I've never written more than three or four in my life, so please forgive me if this one is not what you expected.

As I was leaving the orphanage yesterday, Mrs. Lippett told me to be very respectful to you and to behave well for "the kind gentleman who is doing so much for you."

But how can I be very respectful to a person who wishes to be called John Smith? Why couldn't you have picked out a name with a little personality?

I have been thinking about you. Having someone take an interest in me after all these years makes me feel as though I have found a sort of family. I feel now that at last I belong to someone.

I must say, however, that when I think about you, my imagination has very little to work with. There are just three things that I know about you:

I. You are tall.

II. You are rich.

III. You hate girls.

I would have called you "Dear Mr. Girl Hater," but that would be insulting. Or I could have called you "Dear Mr. Rich Man," but that's insulting to you too, because it implies that money is the most important thing about you. On the other hand, you will stay tall all your life! So I've decided to call you "Dear Daddy-Long-Legs." I hope you won't mind. It's just a private pen name—we won't tell Mrs. Lippett.

The ten o'clock bell is going to ring in two minutes. Our day is divided into sections by bells. We eat and sleep and study by bells. Good night. Observe with what precision I obey rules—due to my training in the John Grier Home.

Yours most affectionately,
Jerusha Abbott

Jerusha writing a letter to Daddy-Long-Legs

To Mr. Daddy-Long-Legs Smith

October 1

Dear Daddy-Long-Legs,

I love college and I love you for sending me. I'm very, very happy and so excited every minute of the day that I can scarcely sleep. You can't imagine how different college is from the John Grier Home. I never dreamed there was such a place in this world. I'm feeling sorry for everybody who isn't a girl and who can't come here. I am sure the college you attended when you were a boy couldn't have been so nice.

My room is up in a tower. There are three other girls on the same floor with me—a senior who wears spectacles and is always asking us to be a little quieter, and two freshmen like me, Sallie McBride and Julia Pendleton. Sallie is quite friendly. Julia comes from one of the first families of New York and hasn't noticed me yet. They room together, but the senior and I have singles. Usually freshmen like me can't get a single room as they are very scarce, but I was lucky to get one without even asking.

After you've lived in an orphanage ward with twenty roommates for eighteen years, it is restful to be alone. This is the first chance I've ever had to get acquainted with myself. I think I'm going to like myself.

Do you like me?

Jerusha Abbott and Sallie McBride

Jerusha Abbott, Sallie McBride and Julia Pendleton

Tuesday

They are organizing the freshmen basketball team, and there's a chance I'll be selected. I'm short of course, but quite quick. While the others are hopping about in the air, I can dodge under their feet and grab the ball. It's loads of fun practicing out in the athletic field in the afternoon.

I meant to write a long letter to you and tell you all the things I'm learning, but the seventh hour has just rung and in ten minutes I'm to assemble at the athletic field in gym clothes. Don't you hope I'll make the team?

Yours always,
Jerusha Abbott

P.S. Nine o'clock

Sallie McBride just poked her head in at the door to tell me she is already feeling homesick. I'm not feeling homesick at all. So at least homesickness is one disease I have escaped! I've never heard of anybody being asylum-sick, have you?

October 10

Dear Daddy-Long-Legs,

Did you ever hear of Michelangelo? He was a famous artist who lived in Italy in the Middle Ages. Everybody in English literature class seemed to know about him and the whole class laughed because I thought he was an angel.

That joke has spread all over the college. The trouble with college is that you are expected to know such a lot of things you've never learned. It's very embarrassing at times. But now, when the girls talk about things that I never heard of, I just keep quiet and look them up in an encyclopedia when I have a chance. Anyway, I'm just as bright in class as any of the others and brighter than some of them!

I went shopping with Sallie McBride to furnish my room. You can't imagine what fun it is for me to pay with a real five-dollar bill *and* to get some change back. When you've never had more than a few cents in your life, five dollars is a large amount of money. I do appreciate the allowance, Daddy dear.

Sallie is the most entertaining person in the world, and Julia Pendleton the least. It's queer what a mixture of roommates one ends up with. Sallie thinks everything is funny—even flunking a test—and Julia is bored with everything. She believes she is superior to all of us because she is a rich Pendleton.

And now I suppose you've been waiting very impatiently to hear what I am learning!

I. Latin: Second Punic War.

II. French: Twenty-four pages of *The Three Musketeers* and third conjunction and irregular verbs.

III. Geometry: Finished cylinders; now doing cones.

IV. English: Studying exposition.

V. Physiology: Reached the digestive system. Bile and the pancreas next time.

Yours on the way to being educated,

Jerusha Abbott

P.S. I hope you never touch alcohol, Daddy! It does dreadful things to your liver.

Wednesday

Dear Daddy-Long-Legs,

I've changed my name.

I'm still Jerusha in the catalog, but I'm Judy everywhere else.

It was Mrs. Lippett who chose my rather unsavory name. She got it from a tombstone. I've always hated it, but I rather like Judy. It's such a silly name. It belongs to the kind of girl I'm not—a sweet little blue-eyed thing, petted and spoilt by all the family, who romps her way through life without any cares. Wouldn't it be nice to be like that?

In the future, please address me as Judy.

[Dinner bell. Goodbye.]

Friday

What do you think, Daddy? The English instructor says that my last paper shows an unusual amount of originality. She truly did; those were her very words. It doesn't seem possible, does it, considering the eighteen years of training that I've had at the asylum?

I hope that I don't hurt your feelings when I criticize the home of my youth. But you have the upper hand, you know, for if I become too impertinent you can always stop payment on your checks. That isn't a very polite thing to say—but you can't expect me to have any manners; a foundling asylum isn't a young ladies' finishing school.

It isn't work and study that is going to be difficult here. It's the conversations. Half the time I don't know what the girls are talking about. I'm a foreigner in the world of young girls brought up in good families. It's a miserable feeling. I've had it all my life, including the time I spent in high school. I could feel "John Grier Home" written all over my face.

Nobody over here knows that I was brought up in an asylum. I told Sallie that my mother and father were dead and that a kind old gentleman was sending me to college, which is entirely true, so far as it goes.

Anyway, Sallie McBride likes me!

Yours ever,
Judy Abbott

October 25

Dear Daddy-Long-Legs,

I'm on the basketball team. Julia Pendleton tried for the team, but she didn't get on. Hurrah!

You see what a mean disposition I have.

College gets nicer and nicer. I like the girls, the teachers, the classes, the campus, and the things we get to eat. We have ice cream twice a week.

You only wanted to hear from me once a month, didn't you? And I have been annoying you with letters every few days! But I've been so excited about all these new adventures that I must talk to somebody, and you're the only one I know. Please excuse my exuberance. I'll settle down soon. If my letters bore you, you can always toss them into the wastebasket. I promise not to write till the middle of November.

Yours lovingly,
Judy Abbott

November 15

Dear Daddy-Long-Legs,

You've never heard about my clothes, have you Daddy? Six dresses, all new and beautiful and bought for me—not handed down from somebody bigger. Perhaps you don't realize what a milestone that marks in the career of an orphan. You gave them to me, and I am very, very much obliged. It's a fine thing to be educated, but nothing compares to the dizzying experience of owning six new dresses. That wouldn't be an awfully big wardrobe for Julia Pendleton perhaps, but for Jerusha Abbott—oh my!

I suppose you're thinking now what a frivolous, shallow little beast I am and what a waste of money to educate a girl.

But, Daddy, if you'd been dressed in checked overalls all your whole life, you'd appreciate how I feel. At high school it was even worse for me. Girls in my class used to donate their old dresses to the poor box for me to wear. You can't know how I dreaded appearing in school in those miserable "poor box dresses." I was always teased and giggled at by the girl who previously owned the dress and pointed them out to the others.

I don't believe I can ever obliterate that scar.

P.S. I know I'm not to expect any letters in return, and I've been warned not to bother you with questions. But tell me, Daddy, are you awfully old or just a little old? And are you perfectly bald or just a little bald? It is very difficult thinking about you in the abstract like a theorem in geometry. What does a tall, rich man who hates girls but is very generous to one quite impertinent girl look like?

December 19

Dear Daddy-Long-Legs,

You never answered my question and it was very important. Are you bald?

I have what you look like very satisfactorily planned out in my head—until I reach the top of your head and then I am stuck. I can't decide whether you have white hair, or black hair, or sort of a sprinkling of gray hair, or maybe no hair at all.

[Chapel bell.]

9:45 p.m.

I have made myself a new, unbreakable rule to never study at night no matter how many written reviews are coming in the morning. Instead, I just read plain books—I have to, you know, because there are eighteen blank years behind me. You wouldn't believe, Daddy, what an abyss of ignorance my mind is; I am just realizing now how ignorant I am. The things that most girls with a proper family, and a home, and friends, and a library, know by absorption, I have never heard of.

For example: I never read *Mother Goose,* or *David Copperfield,* or *Ivanhoe,* or *Cinderella,* or *Blue Beard,* or *Robinson Crusoe,* or *Jane Eyre,* or *Alice in Wonderland,* or a word of Rudyard Kipling. I didn't know that Henry the Eighth was married more than once or that Shelley was a poet. I didn't know that people used to be monkeys and that the Garden of Eden was a beautiful myth. I didn't know that R.L.S. stood for Robert Louis Stevenson or that George Eliot was a lady. I had never seen a picture of the Mona Lisa, and (it's true, but you won't believe it) I had never heard of Sherlock Holmes.

Now I know all of these things and a lot more, but you can see how much I need to catch up. And, oh, but it's fun! All day I look forward to the evening and then I put an "engaged" sign on the door and get into my nice red bathrobe and furry slippers, and I pile all the cushions behind me on the couch, light the brass student lamp at my elbow, and read and read. One book isn't enough. I have four going at once. Just now, they're Tennyson's poems and *Vanity Fair* and Kipling's *Plain Tales* and—don't laugh—*Little Women*. I find that I am the only girl in college who wasn't brought up on *Little Women*. I haven't told anybody, though. I just quietly bought it with $1.12 of my last month's allowance.

[Ten o'clock bell. This is a very interrupted letter.]

Jrusha Abbott making up for eighteen years of ignorance

Sunday

The Christmas vacation begins next week, and every girl is going home for the holidays except one other freshman and me. We are planning to take long walks, and if there's any ice we will learn to skate. Then there is still the whole library to be read and three empty weeks to do it in!

Goodbye till January—and Merry Christmas!

Yours ever,
Judy

Toward the end of the Christmas vacation. Exact date unknown.

Dear Daddy-Long-Legs,

Your five gold pieces were a surprise! I'm not used to receiving Christmas presents. You have already given me such a lot of things—everything I have, you know?—that I don't feel I deserve extras. But I like them all the same! Do you want to know what I bought with my money?

I. A silver watch in a leather case to wear on my wrist and get me to recitation on time.

II. Mathew Arnold's poems.

III. A steamer rug. (My tower is cold.)

IV. Five hundred sheets of yellow manuscript paper. (I'm going to commence being an author pretty soon.)

V. A dictionary of synonyms. (To enlarge the author's vocabulary.)

VI. (I don't much like to confess this last item; but I will) A pair of silk stockings.

And now, Daddy—never say I don't tell all!

It was a very low motive, if you must know, that prompted the silk stockings. Julia Pendleton comes into my room to do geometry and she sits cross-legged on the couch and wears silk stockings every night. But just wait! As soon as she gets back from vacation, I shall go in and sit on her couch in my silk stockings. You see, Daddy, the miserable creature that I am, but at least I'm honest and you knew already from my asylum record that I wasn't perfect, didn't you?

So you see, Daddy, my education progresses!

Don't you really think I ought to be an artist instead of an author?

Vacation will be over in two days, and I shall be glad to see the girls again. My tower is a trifle lonely, when nine people occupy a house that was built for four hundred. They do rattle around a bit.

I meant that to be a short little thank-you note, but when I get started, I seem to have a ready pen.

Goodbye and thank you for thinking of me. I should be perfectly happy except for one little threatening cloud on the horizon. Examinations come in February.

Yours with love,
Judy

P.S. Maybe it isn't proper to send love? If it isn't, please excuse me. But I must love somebody, and there's only you and Mrs. Lippett to choose between, so you see? You'll have to put up with it, Daddy dear, because I can't love her.

On the eve of the exams

Dear Daddy-Long-Legs,

You should see the way this college is studying! We've forgotten we ever had a vacation. I have introduced fifty-seven irregular verbs to my brain these past four days. I'm only hoping they'll stay till after examinations.

Some of the girls sell their textbooks when they're through with them, but I intend to keep mine. After I've graduated I shall have my whole education in the bookcase, and when I need to remember any detail, I can turn to it without the slightest hesitation. So much easier and more accurate than trying to keep it in your head.

I meant to write you a nice cheerful, entertaining letter but I'm too sleepy—and scared. The freshman's lot is not a happy one.

Yours about to be examined,
Judy Abbott

Sunday

Dearest Daddy-Long-Legs,

I have some awful, awful, awful news to tell you, but I won't begin with it. I'll try to get you in a good humor first.

Jerusha Abbott has commenced to be an author. A poem entitled "From My Tower" appears in the February *Monthly*, on the first page, which is a very great honor for a freshman. I shall send you a copy in case you care to read it.

Now for the news—courage, Judy!—you must tell.

Are you surely in a good humor? I failed in mathematics and Latin prose. I am getting tutored in them and will take another examination next month. I am sorry if you're disappointed, but otherwise I don't care a bit because I've learned such a lot of things not mentioned in the catalog. I've read seventeen novels and bushels of poetry—really necessary novels like *Vanity Fair* and *Richard Feverel* and *Alice in Wonderland*.

So you see, Daddy, I'm much more intelligent than if I'd just stuck to Latin. Will you forgive me this once, if I promise never to flunk again?

Yours in sackcloth,
Judy

Dear Daddy-Long-Legs,

This is an extra letter in the middle of the month because I'm sort of lonely tonight. It's awfully starry;

the snow is beating against my tower. All the lights are out on the campus, but I drank black coffee and I can't go to sleep.

I had a supper party this evening with Sallie and Julia. We had sardines, toasted muffins, salad, fudge, and coffee. Julia said she'd had a good time, and Sallie stayed up to help wash the dishes.

I might very usefully put some time on Latin tonight—but, there's no doubt about it. I'm a very languid Latin scholar.

That's the chapel tower striking twelve. I believe I am sleepy after all.

Good night.
I love you dearly,
Judy

The Ides of March
March 13

Dear D.L.L.,

I am studying Latin prose composition. My reexamination comes next Tuesday, and I am going to pass or BUST. So, you may expect to hear from me next—whole and happy, and free from conditions—or in fragments.

I will write a respectable letter when it's over.

Yours in evident haste,
J.A.

March 26

Mr. D. -L. -L. Smith,

Sir: You never answer any questions. You never show the slightest interest in anything I do. You are probably the most horrid of all those horrid trustees, and the reason you are educating me is not because you care a bit about me, but from a sense of duty.

I don't know a single thing about you. I don't even know your name. It is very uninspiring writing to a "thing." I haven't a doubt that you throw my letters into the wastebasket without reading them. Hereafter, I shall write only about work.

My re-exams in Latin and geometry were last week. I passed them both and am now free from conditions.

Yours truly,
Jerusha Abbott

April 2

Dear Daddy-Long-Legs,

I am a BEAST!

Please forget about that dreadful letter I sent you last week. I was feeling lonely and miserable and sore throaty the night I wrote it. I didn't know it, but I was just coming down with tonsillitis, grippe, and lots of things all mixed together. I'm in the infirmary now and have been for six days. This is the first time they let me sit up and have a pen and paper. I've been thinking about my awful letter all the time, and I shan't get well until you forgive me.

Doesn't all of this arouse your sympathy? I am suffering from sublingual gland swelling. And I've been studying physiology all the year without so much as hearing about sublingual glands. How futile a thing is education!

I can't write anymore. I get sort of shaky when I sit up for too long. Please forgive me for being callous and so ungrateful. I was badly brought up.

Yours with love,
Judy Abbott

The Infirmary,
April 4

Dear Daddy-Long-Legs,

Yesterday evening the nurse appeared with a long white box addressed to me and filled with the loveliest pink rosebuds along with a card from you. Your handwriting shows that you're a man with a great deal of character. Thank you, Daddy, a thousand times. Your flowers make the first true present I ever received in my life. If you want to know what a baby I am, I lay down and cried because I was so happy.

Now I am sure you read my letters, and I'll make them so interesting they'll be worth keeping in a safe. Only please take out that dreadful one and burn it up. I hate to think that you might one day read it over.

Thank you for making a very sick freshman cheerful. Probably you have lots of loving family and friends, and you don't know what it feels like to be alone. But I do.

Goodbye. I promise never to be horrid again because now I know that you are a real person. Also, I promise never to bother you with any more questions.

Do you still hate girls?

Yours forever,
Judy

After chapel, Thursday

Dear Daddy-Long-Legs,

What do you think is my favorite book? Just now, I mean; I change every three days. *Wuthering Heights*. Emily Bronte was quite young when she wrote it and had never been outside of Haworth Churchyard. She had never known any men in her life. How could she imagine a man like Heathcliff?

I couldn't do it, and I'm quite young and have never been outside the John Grier Asylum.

Sometimes a dreadful fear comes over me, and I fear that I'm not a genius. Will you be awfully disappointed, Daddy, if I don't turn out to be an author? In fact, it's much more entertaining to read books than to write them. Ow!!!

A centipede just fell off the ceiling and landed by my side as I wrote this last line. Sallie and Julia came in to help me kill it when they heard my cry. This dormitory, owing to its age and ivy-covered walls is full of centipedes. They are dreadful creatures. I'd rather find a tiger under my bed.

May 27

Daddy-Long-Legs, Esq.

Dear Sir,

I am in receipt of a letter from Mrs. Lippett. She hopes that I am doing well in behavior and studies. Since I probably have no place to go this summer, she will let me come back to the asylum and work for my board until college reopens.

I HATE THE JOHN GRIER HOME.

I'd rather die than go back.

Yours most truthfully,

Jerusha Abbott

May 30

Dear Daddy-Long-Legs,

I'm glad I'm being sent by you to a farm instead of to the John Grier Home. I am very, very grateful to you and thank you profusely. This summer I'm going to write and write, and begin to be a great author.

I wish you'd come for a little visit to my college campus. I could show you around, as the campus looks very beautiful during spring.

Mr. Jervie Pendleton

Oh, I'm fine at showing people around. I've done it all my life at the asylum and I'm good at doing it here too.

I must inform you, I've at last conversed with a man. In fact, I have been walking and talking and having tea with a man! Something that I've never done all my life. His name is Mr. Jervie Pendleton of the House of Julia; her uncle in short. However, he is as tall as you are. Being in town on business, he decided to come to the campus and visit his brother's daughter—that is, Julia. Julia doesn't know much about him other than the fact that he is her father's youngest brother.

Anyway, there he was, sitting in the reception room, very proper with his hat, stick, and gloves besides him. Julia was busy at recitations, so she begged me to keep her uncle company, something I did not want to do; after all, I don't care much for the Pendletons.

But he turned out to be a sweet lamb. He's a real human being—not a Pendleton at all—and we had a beautiful time.

He is tall, on the thinner side, and has a very charming smile. He has a way of making you feel right off as though you'd known him a long time. He's very companionable.

Jerusha Abbott shows Mr. Jervie Pendleton the whole campus

I showed him the whole campus and then he took me to an inn to have tea, muffins, marmalade, and ice cream.

We spoke a lot and had the jolliest time, but he had to run for his train and so he barely saw Julia at all. She is furious with me for taking him away, as it seems he's an unusually rich uncle. It relieved my mind to find he was rich, for the tea and things cost sixty cents apiece.

This morning, Julia, Sallie, and I received boxes of chocolate from him. What do you think of that? A man sending me candy!

I wish you'd come and take me to tea someday and let me see if I like you.

Yours with love,
Judy

June 9

Dear Daddy-Long-Legs,

Happy day! I've just finished my last examination, which was physiology, and now I'll be spending three months on a farm!

I've never been on a farm in my whole life. In fact, I've never been anywhere outside the John Grier Home. Whenever I think of my holiday, excited little thrills chase up and down my back.

I leave you now, to pack a trunk.

Yours ever,
Judy

Saturday night

Dearest Daddy-Long-Legs,

I've only just come and I've not yet unpacked. But I can't wait to tell you how much I like the farm. This is a heavenly, heavenly, heavenly spot! The house where I am staying is square and very old, about a hundred years.

It's called Lock Willow Farm, and I like it very much. The people here are Mr. and Mrs. Semple, a hired girl, and two hired men. We had ham, jelly cakes, pie, and pickles to eat, and a great conversation to entertain us. There is a big, square mahogany table in the room where I sleep. I'm going to spend my summer with my elbows spread out on it, writing a novel.

Oh, Daddy, I'm so excited! I can't wait till daylight to begin exploring. It's 8:30 p.m. now, and I am about to blow out my candle and try to go to sleep. We rise at five.

Good night,
Judy

P.S. You should hear the frogs sing and the little pigs squeal.

Lock Willows
July 12

Dear Daddy-Long-Legs,

Listen to this: Mr. Jervie Pendleton used to own this farm, but he has since given it to Mrs. Semple, who amazingly was his old nurse. Did you ever hear of such a funny coincidence? She still calls him "Master Jervie" and talks about what a sweet little boy he used to be.

Since she discovered that I know him, I have risen very much in her opinion. He happens to be the cream of the Pendleton family.

It is my daily business, here at the farm, to gather the eggs. While doing so, I fell off a beam and scratched my knee. Mrs. Semple was spreading ointment on my wound, saying it seemed like just yesterday that Master Jervie had scratched that very same knee.

The scenery around here is perfectly beautiful. We have many cows and pigs.

I haven't had time yet to begin my immortal novel, as the farm keeps me too busy.

Yours always,
Judy

Jerusha finds areal dadddy long legs spider on her writing desk

Sunday

Dear Daddy-Long-Legs,

Yesterday on my writing desk at Lock Willow, I found a real daddy long legs spider. I picked him up very gently by one leg and dropped him out of the window. I wouldn't hurt one of them for the world. They always remind me of you.

In two more minutes when this letter is finished, I am going to settle down to a book I found in the attic. It's entitled *On the Trail* and scrawled across the front page in a funny little boy's hand are the following words:

Jervie Pendleton
"If this book should ever roam,
Box its ears and send it home."

He spent the summer here once after he had been ill when he was eleven years old and he left *On the Trail* behind. It looks well read—the marks of his grimy little hands are frequent. Mrs. Semple doesn't think of him as a grown man but as a young little boy still.

I've gained a lot of weight after coming to Lock Willow.

Sir,
I remain,
Your affectionate orphan,
Judy Abbott

Jerusha Abbott with her roommates, Sallie McBride and Julia Pendleton

September 25,

Dear Daddy-Long-Legs,

Behold me—a sophomore! I came back last Friday, sorry to leave Lock Willow but glad to see the campus again. It is a pleasant sensation to come back to something familiar. I am beginning, in fact, to feel at home in the world—as though I really belong in it.

And now, Daddy, listen to this. Whom do you think I am rooming with? Sallie McBride and Julia Pendleton. It's the truth. We have a study and three little bedrooms. Think of Jerusha Abbott from the John Grier Home for Orphans rooming with a Pendleton! This is indeed a democratic country.

Sallie is running for class president, and I do hope she wins. Elections are next Saturday.

I am beginning to study chemistry, and it is a very unusual subject. I am also studying logic, the plays of William Shakespeare, the history of the whole world, and French. If this keeps up for many years longer, I shall become quite intelligent.

Yours always,

J. Abbott

October 17

Dear Daddy-Long-Legs,

Did I ever tell you about the election? It happened three weeks ago. Sallie was elected, and we had a torchlight parade.

We're very important people now in room 258. Julia and I receive a great deal of reflected glory. It's quite a social strain to be living in the same house with a president.

With all my love,
Judy

November 12

Dear Daddy-Long-Legs,

Sallie has invited me to spend the Christmas vacation with her and her family. She lives in Worcester, Massachusetts. Wasn't it nice of her? I shall love to go. I've never stayed with a private family in my life except at Lock Willow. Sallie has a sister and two brothers, a mother, a father, a grandmother, and a cat. It's a perfectly complete family! Packing a trunk and going away is more fun than staying behind. I'm terribly excited at the prospect.

Yours with all my love,
J.A.

I had a glorius time dancing with Jimmie McBride

Stone Gate,
Worcester, Massachusetts,
December 31

Dear Daddy-Long-Legs,

I meant to write to you before and thank you for your Christmas check, but life in the McBride household is very absorbing. I've been having the most beautiful vacation visiting Sallie. Everything is so comfortable and restful and homelike.

Sallie's older brother, named Jimmie, is a junior at the Princeton College. We have the jolliest times at the table—everyone laughs and jokes and talks at once.

We all went for a dance, and my partner was Jimmie McBride. I had such a glorious time dancing.

Yours ever,
Judy Abbott

P.S. Would you be terribly displeased, Daddy, if I didn't turn out to be a Great Author after all, but just a Plain Girl?

6:30 p.m.
Saturday

Dear Daddy,

It has been raining a lot today, and who do you think showed up at the college but Julia's uncle. He brought a five-pound box of chocolates for us. You see? There are advantages to rooming with Julia.

He wanted to stay and have tea with us, but Julia had a lot of trouble getting permission for Mr. Jervie Pendleton to stay for a while from the dormitory officials. You see, he is very youngish and good looking.

Anyway, permission was granted, and we had our tea along with cheese and sandwiches. I told him I had spent last summer at Lock Willow, and we had a beautiful, gossipy time about the Semples and the horses, cows, and chickens. All the horses that he used to know are dead, except for Grover, who was just a colt at the time of his last visit—and poor Grover is so old now, he can do no more than limp about the pasture.

I called him "Master Jervie" to his face, but he didn't appear to be insulted. Julia says that she has never seen him so amiable. Apparently he is usually pretty unapproachable.

Mercy, how it keeps pouring! We shall have to swim to chapel tonight.

Yours ever,
Judy

February 4

Dear Daddy-Long-Legs,

Jimmie McBride has sent me a Princeton College banner as big as one end of the room. I am very grateful to him for remembering me, but I don't know what on earth to do with it. Sallie and Julia won't let me hang it up. But it's such a nice, warm, thick felt, I'd hate to waste it. Would it be very improper to have it made into a bathrobe? My old one shrank last it was washed.

Lately I've failed to tell you what I am learning, and though you might not imagine it from my letters, my time is exclusively occupied with study.

Sixth-hour-bell—I must go to the laboratory and look into a little matter of acids, salts, and alkalis. I've burnt a hole as big as a plate in the front of my chemistry apron with hydrochloric acid. If the theory proves true, then I ought to neutralize that hole with good strong ammonia, oughtn't I?

Examinations next week, but who's afraid?

Yours ever,
Judy

March 5

Dear Daddy-Long-Legs,

There is a March wind blowing, and the sky is filled with heavy, black, moving clouds. The winds make an intoxicating, exhilarating, "calling" noise. You'd want to close your books and be off over the hills to race with it.

I never told you about examinations. I passed everything with the utmost ease. I know the secret of studying now and am never going to flunk again. However, I shan't be able to graduate with honors, because of that beastly Latin prose and geometry freshman year.

Speaking of studies, have you ever read the play *Hamlet*? If you haven't, then do it right now. It's simply wonderful. I've been hearing about Shakespeare all my life but I had no idea he wrote so well. I always suspected him of going largely on his reputation.

I must continue to read it.

I remain sir,
Yours most graciously,
Jerusha A.

March 24

Dear Daddy-Long-Legs,

I don't believe I can be going to Heaven—I am getting so many good things here, it wouldn't be fair to get them hereafter too. Listen to what has happened.

Jerusha Abbott, that's me, has won the short story contest (a twenty-five-dollar prize) that the *Monthly* holds every year. And I am only a sophomore! The contestants are mainly seniors. When I saw my name posted, I couldn't quite believe it was true. Maybe I am going to be an author after all.

Also, I have been chosen for the spring dramatics—*As You Like It* by William Shakespeare—which will be held outdoors. I am playing the role of Celia, cousin to the lead heroine.

And lastly: Julia, Sallie, and I are going to New York next Friday to do some spring shopping and stay overnight. We will also attend the theater the following day, with Master Jervie. He invited us. Did you ever hear of anything so exciting? I've never been in a hotel in my life, nor in a theater, except once when the Church had a festival and invited the orphans, but that wasn't a real play and it doesn't count.

And what do you think we are going to see? *Hamlet*. Think of that! We studied it for four weeks in Shakespeare class, and I know it by heart.

I am so very excited about all of these prospects that I can scarcely sleep.

Goodbye Daddy.

This is a very entertaining world.

Yours ever,
Judy

P.S. I saw a streetcar conductor today with one brown eye and one blue. Wouldn't he make a nice and proper villain for a detective story?

April 7

Dear Daddy-Long-Legs,

Mercy! Isn't New York big? Do you mean to tell me that you actually live in all that confusion? I don't believe I shall recover for months from the bewildering effect of being there for just two days. I can't begin to tell you all the amazing things I've seen, but I suppose you know it all since you live there yourself.

But aren't the streets entertaining? And the people? And the shops? I never saw such lovely things as I saw in the shop windows of New York City. They make you want to devote your life to wearing clothes!

Julia bought two very expensive hats without even looking at the price tag. I hope that one day I will also be able to do that.

After we finished shopping, we met Master Jervie at Sherry's. I ate my fish with the wrong fork, but the waiter very kindly gave me another so that nobody noticed.

And after luncheon we went to the theater. It was dazzling and marvelous, and I dream about it every night.

Isn't Shakespeare wonderful?

Hamlet is so much better on the stage than when we analyzed it in class.

I wish I could be an actress instead of an author. Wouldn't you like me to leave college and go into a dramatic school? And then I'll send you a box ticket for all of my performances and smile at you across the footlights. Be sure to wear a red rose in your button-hole, please, so I'm sure to smile at the right man. It would be an awfully embarrassing mistake if I smiled at the wrong one.

Master Jervie gave Sallie, Julia, and me each a bunch of violets and lilies of the valley. Wasn't that sweet of him? I never used to care much for men—judging by the trustees I've met—but I'm changing my mind.

Yours always,
Judy

April 10

Dear Mr. Rich Man,

Here's your check for fifty dollars. Thank you very much, but I do not feel that I can keep it. My allowance is sufficient to afford all the hats I need. I am sorry that I wrote all that silly stuff about the shopping and the hats; it's just that I had never seen anything like it before.

However, I wasn't begging! And I would rather not accept any more charity than I have to.

Sincerely yours,
Jerusha Abbott

April 11

Dearest Daddy,

Will you please forgive me for the letter I wrote you yesterday? After I posted it, I was sorry and tried to get it back, but that beastly mail clerk wouldn't give it to me.

It's the middle of the night now. I've been awake for hours thinking of what a worm I am. I've closed the door very softly to the study so as not to wake Julia and Sallie, and am sitting up in bed writing to you on paper torn out of my history notebook.

I just wanted to tell you that I am sorry I was so impatient about your check. I know you meant it kindly and I think you're an old dear to take so much trouble for such a silly thing as a hat. I ought to have returned it much more graciously.

You'll forgive me, won't you, for being so rude? I have an awful habit of writing impulsively when I first think things and then posting a letter beyond recall. But if I sometimes seem thoughtless and ungrateful, I never mean it. In my heart, I thank you always for the life, freedom, and independence that you have given me. I am so happy because of you that I feel like a made-up heroine in a storybook.

It's a quarter past two. I'm going to tiptoe out and post this off now. You'll receive it in the next mail after the other, so you won't have a long time to think badly of me.

Goodnight, Daddy.

I love you always,
Judy

May 4

Dear Daddy-Long-Legs,

It was Field Day last Saturday, a spectacular occasion. Julia dressed up for the parade as a fat country man with whiskers and a baggy umbrella. She played the part extremely well. I never dreamt that a Pendleton could display so much comic spirit—begging Master Jervie's pardon. I don't consider him a true Pendleton, though, any more than I consider you a true trustee.

Sallie and I weren't in the parade because we were entered in the events. And how do you think we did in those events? We both won! Sallie won the pole vaulting (seven feet, three inches), and I won the fifty-yard sprint (eight seconds).

I sat up half of last night reading *Jane Eyre*. Are you old enough, Daddy, to remember sixty years ago? And if so, did people talk that way? *Jane Eyre* is melodrama in the purest sense, but you can't help but read, and read, and read it.

You know, Daddy, I think that the most necessary quality for any person to have is imagination. It allows people to put themselves in other peoples' places. It ought to be cultivated in children.

(There goes the chapel bell. I'll finish this letter sometime.)

Judy

June 2

Dear Daddy-Long-Legs,

You will never guess the nicest thing that has happened. The McBrides have asked me to spend the summer at their camp in the Adirondacks! It's going to be so much fun. Jimmie McBride is going to have a college friend visiting him part of the summer, so we shall have plenty of men for dancing partners.

Wasn't it sweet of Mrs. McBride to ask me? It appears that she liked me when I was there for Christmas.

Please excuse this letter for being too short. It isn't a real letter; it's just to let you know that I'm disposed of for the summer.

Yours hastily,
Judy

June 5

Dear Daddy-Long-Legs,

Your secretary has just written to me with the message that Mr. Smith prefers that I decline Mrs. McBride's invitation and that I should return to Lock Willow the same as last summer.

Why, why, why, Daddy?

You don't understand. Mrs. McBride does want me to stay, really and truly. I'm not going to be trouble for her. In fact, she is going to teach me housekeeping. Being with Mrs. McBride is an education in itself.

Jerusha cries as she writes a letter to Daddy-Long-Legs

Also, Mrs. McBride wants me for a companion for Sallie. We are planning to do a lot of reading together. We are going to read all of the books for next year's English and sociology.

Also, Jimmie McBride is going to teach me how to ride horseback and paddle a canoe and how to shoot and—oh, lots of things that I ought to know.

Of course, I'll do exactly as you say, but please, PLEASE let me go, Daddy. I've never wanted anything so much. This isn't Jerusha Abbott the future great author writing to you. It's just Judy—a girl.

Yours with love,
J. Abbott

June 9

Mr. John Smith,

Sir: In compliance with the instructions received through your secretary, I leave on Friday next to spend the summer at Lock Willow Farm.

I hope to always remain,
(Miss) Jerusha Abbott

Lock Willow Farm,
August 3

Dear Daddy-Long-Legs,

It has been nearly two months since I wrote, which wasn't nice of me, I know, but I haven't loved you much this summer. You see, I'm being frank!

I was very disappointed because I couldn't go to the McBrides' for the summer break. Of course, I know that you're my guardian and that I have to regard your wishes in all matters, but I couldn't see ANY REASON for it!

The impersonality of your commands hurt my feelings. I know I was to write nice, long detailed letters without ever expecting an answer. You're living up to your side of the bargain, and I suppose you're thinking that I'm not living up to mine!

But, Daddy, you are so shadowy and mysterious. Sometimes I think you are not the kind and lovely man I've always thought you to be. But then I remember the rosebuds and card you sent me when I was in the infirmary, and I remember that you do care. I still have your card, and I read it over and over again when I am lonely and when I feel that I don't have a family.

I've been writing and writing this summer: four short stories that I've sent to four different magazines. So, you see, I'm trying to be an author.

Yours as ever,
Judy

August 10

Dear Daddy-Long-Legs,

If you are in that dreadful New York, I wish I could send you some of this lovely, breezy, sunshiny optimism. The country is heaven after a week of rain.

During our week of rain, I sat up in the attic and partook in an orgy of reading—Stevenson mostly. He is more entertaining than any of the characters in his books. Don't you think it was perfect of him to spend the whole ten thousand dollars his father left him on a yacht, which he sailed into the South Seas? He lived up to his adventurous creed. If my father had left me ten thousand dollars, I'd do it too. I want to see the whole world. I am going to someday when I get to be a great author.

Good night,
Judy

Friday

Good morning! Here is some news! Mrs. Semple got a letter from Mr. Jervie Pendleton saying that he was coming to spend a few weeks here at Lock Willow Farm.

We are all in such a flutter after we've got the news. The whole house is being cleaned and all the curtains washed.

But isn't it just like a man, Daddy? He didn't give us the exact date when he would be arriving. Thus, we shall live in perpetual breathlessness until he comes.

With my hand on my heart—farewell!

Judy

P.S. Isn't that a nice ending? I got it out of Stevenson's letters.

August 25

Dear Daddy-Long-Legs,

Well, Daddy, Master Jervie is here, and we are having such a nice time! At least I am, and I think he is too. He has been here ten days and doesn't show any signs of leaving. The way Mrs. Semple pampers that man is scandalous. If she indulged him as much when he was a baby, I don't know how he ever turned out so well.

He is an awfully companionable sort of man and talks to all farmers not like a rich man, but in a very respectful and friendly manner. His clothes, however, are very rich and whenever he comes down from his room wearing a new suit, Mrs. Semple beams with pride and walks around him, viewing him from every angle.

He is always saying to her, "Run along, Lizzie, and tend to your work. You can't boss me any longer. I've grown up."

It's awfully funny to think of that great big, long-legged man ever sitting in Mrs. Semple's lap and having his face washed.

Such a lot of adventure we're having! We've explored the country for miles, and I've learned to fish, shoot a rifle, and a revolver, and to ride on horseback.

Master Jervie has read all the books I've ever read and a lot of others besides. It's astonishing how many different things he knows.

Jerusha and Mr. Jervie Pendleton getting wet in the rain

We came in this morning drenched due to the storm, and you should have seen Mrs. Semple's face when we dripped into her kitchen. She was funny.

I've tried asking Mr. Pendleton whether he knows you, as you both move in the same city and social circles, but I couldn't get far obviously, because I don't know your real name. It's the silliest thing, not to know your name. Mrs. Lippett warned me that you were eccentric, and I think so too!

Affectionately,
Judy

September 10

Dear Daddy,

He has gone, and we are missing him! When you get accustomed to people, or places, or ways of living and then have them suddenly snatched away, it does leave an awfully empty gnawing sort of sensation.

College opens in two weeks, and I shall be glad to begin work again. I have worked quite a lot this summer, though—I wrote a total of six short stories and seven poems. It's good practice. Master Jervie read them, and he felt they all were dreadful. Master Jervie doesn't let politeness interfere with truth. But the last one I did—just a little sketch on college life—he said wasn't bad, and he had it typewritten and I sent it to a magazine. They've had it two weeks; maybe they're thinking it over.

You should see the sky! There's the queerest orange-colored light over everything. We're going to have a storm.

Thursday

Daddy! Daddy! What do you think? The postman has come with two letters.

First—My story is accepted. $50. I am an AUTHOR.

Second—A letter from the college secretary. I'm to have a scholarship for two years that will cover board and tuition. It was for "marked proficiency in English with general excellency in other lines"—and I've won it! I applied for it before I left, but I didn't have an idea I'd get it on account of my bad freshman work in math and Latin. But it seems I've made it up. I am awfully glad, Daddy, because now I won't be such a burden to you. The monthly allowance will be all I need, and maybe I can earn that with writing or tutoring or something.

I am crazy to go back and begin work.

Yours ever,
Jerusha Abbott

Author of: "When the Sophomores Won the Game."
For sale at all newsstands, price ten cents.

September 26,

Dear Daddy-Long-Legs,

I'm back at the college again and an upper classman. Our study is better than ever this year. We have new wallpaper and Oriental rugs and mahogany chairs.

And, Daddy, I found your secretary's letter waiting for me telling me not to accept the scholarship.

Will you kindly convey to me a comprehensible reason why I should not accept that scholarship? I don't understand your objection in the least. Anyway, I've already accepted it—and I am not going to change. I don't want to spend the rest of my life paying debts. I am aware that you don't want me to return your money, but I will as it is the right thing to do.

I hope you understand my position and won't be cross. The allowance I shall most gratefully accept.

Goodnight, Daddy dear, and don't be annoyed because your chick is wanting to scratch for herself. She's growing up into an awfully energetic little hen with a very determined cluck and lots of beautiful feathers, all due to you.

Affectionately,

Judy

September 30

Dear Daddy,

Are you still harping on that scholarship? I never knew a man so stubborn and unreasonable and unable to see other people's point of view.

You say in your curt letter that I shouldn't accept the scholarship of strangers. Strangers!—And what are you then? Is there any doubt that you are as good a stranger to me as anyone? I shouldn't recognize you if I met you in the street.

And besides, this isn't a favor; it's like a prize I've earned with my hard work. If my work in English wasn't outstanding, the committee wouldn't have awarded me the scholarship.

I refuse, sir, to give up the scholarship; and if you make any more fuss, I won't accept the monthly allowance you give me, either.

That is my ultimatum!

Yours
With a mind made up,
Jerusha Abbott

November 9

Dear Daddy-Long-Legs,

Julia Pendleton has invited me to visit her for the Christmas holidays. How does that strike you, Mr. Smith? Fancy, Jerusha Abbott of the John Grier Home sitting at the tables of the rich. I don't know why Julia wants me—she seems to be getting quite attached to me of late. I should, to tell the truth, very much prefer going to Sallie's, but Julia asked me first. So, if I go anywhere, it must be to New York.

I have elected economics this year, and it is a very illuminating subject. When I finish that, I'm going to take Charity and Reform and then, Mr. Trustee, I'll know just how an orphan asylum ought to be run.

By the by, I was twenty-one last week.

Yours always,
Judy

December 20

Dear Daddy-Long-Legs,

I've just a moment because I must attend two classes, pack a trunk and a suitcase, and catch the four o'clock train—but I could not go without sending a word to let you know how much I appreciate my Christmas box.

I love the furs, necklace, liberty scarf, gloves, handkerchiefs, and books—and most of all, I love you! Daddy, you have no business to spoil me this way. I'm only human. How can I keep my mind sternly fixed on a studious career when you deflect me with such worldly frivolities?

I have strong suspicions now as to which of the John Grier trustees used to give the Christmas tree and the Sunday ice cream. He was nameless, but by his works I know him. You deserve to be happy for all the good things you do.

Goodbye, and a very merry Christmas to you.

Yours always,
Judy

January 11

Dear Daddy-Long-Legs,

I meant to write to you from the city, but New York is an engrossing place.

I had an interesting and illuminating time with the Pendletons, but I'm glad I don't belong in such a family.

Mrs. Pendleton never thinks of anything but jewels, dressmakers, and social engagements. She seems a different kind of mother from Mrs. McBride! If I ever marry and have a family, I'm going to make it as much like the McBrides' as I can. Not for all the money in the world would I ever let any child of mine develop into Pendletons. Maybe it isn't polite to criticize people you've been visiting? If it isn't, please excuse me and let's keep it a secret between you and me.

I saw Master Jervie only once in that house, for tea. The rest of the family thinks him unbalanced. He is not like them at all.

I'm glad to get back to college and my books. The books, study, and regular classes keep me alert mentally, and my friends keep me in congenial company.

Yours ever,
Judy

February 11

Dear D.L.L.,

Don't be insulted because this is so short. It isn't a letter. It's just a line to say that I'm going to write a letter pretty soon when examinations are over. It is not only necessary that I pass, but pass WELL. I have a scholarship to live up to.

Yours studying hard,
J.A.

March ___

My dear Mr. Smith,

You will be pleased to hear that I passed my mid-year examinations successfully and am now commencing work for the new semester. I'm leaving chemistry and am entering upon the study of biology. I approach this subject with some hesitation, as I understand that we dissect angleworms and frogs. We are reading Wordsworth's poems in connection with

Jerusha dancing with Jimmie McBride

our course in English literature, and what an exquisite work are his poems.

I am attending a gymnasium very regularly of late. The gymnasium is equipped with a swimming pool, so I am learning how to swim. Sallie McBride lent me her old swimming suit to wear, as it had shrunk and no longer fits her.

We had delicious pink ice cream for dessert last night.

Trusting my dear Mr. Smith that this will find you in your usual good health.

I remain,
Most cordially yours,
Judy Abbott

April 24

Dear Daddy,

Spring has come again! You should see how lovely the campus is. I think you must come and look at it for yourself. Master Jervie dropped in again last Friday, but he chose a most unpropitious time. Sallie, Julia, and I were going to Princeton College to attend a dance and ball game with Jimmie McBride and his college mates. Mrs. McBride came with us, and we all had a charming time.

Affectionately,
Judy

May 15,

Dear Daddy-Long-Legs,

I should have written and finished this letter a long time ago. You don't mind if I am a bit irregular, do you, Daddy? I really do love to write to you. It gives such a respectable feeling of having some family. Would you like me to tell you something? You are not the only man to whom I write letters. There are two others! Master Jervie writes nice, long letters to me, and short little letters written on yellow pad come from Jimmie McBride. So, you see? I am not so different from other girls; I get mail, too.

There goes the gong for dinner. I'll mail this as I pass the box.

Affectionately,

J

June 10

Dear Daddy-Long-Legs,

I am very busy with examinations and much studying. Sallie wants me to vacation with her at Camp McBride in the Adirondacks this year. And because I feel like taking a little healthful recreation, and I want to see the Adirondacks, and I want to see Sallie's brother, I will be going this year. Jimmie is going to teach me to canoe. My chief motive for going to Camp McBride is that I want to be free and yet feel like I'm part of a family. You cannot dictate to me any other order, dear Daddy. After the examinations, I'm off!

Yours always,
Judy

Camp McBride,
September 6

Dear Daddy,

As you observe, I'm here at camp and I have been here for a number of weeks. As I knew he would, your secretary sent me a lot of mail in an attempt to dissuade me from going to Camp McBride—the letters tempted me with the prospect of going to Europe for the holidays, but I left the college just in time.

The woods are fine and so is the camp. The McBrides have been wonderful and I'm very happy!

There's Jimmie calling for me to come canoeing. Goodbye and sorry to have disobeyed.

However, I love you still, Daddy, in spite of your faults.

Judy

October 3

Dear Daddy-Long-Legs,

I'm back at college, a senior and also editor of the *Monthly*. It doesn't seem possible, does it, that so sophisticated a person just four years ago was an inmate of the John Grier Home? We do arrive fast in America!

What do you think of this? I've received a note from Master Jervie directed to the college. He hopes I've had a nice summer and am enjoying the country. And he knew all the time that I was with the McBrides, for Julia told him so!

Julia had a trunkful of the most ravishing new clothes befitting the angels in Paradise.

Dear Daddy, aren't you glad you're not a girl? I suppose you think the fuss we make over clothes is too absolutely silly. No doubt about it, it is, but it's entirely your fault.

Yours ever,
Judy

November 17

Dear Daddy-Long-Legs,

Such a blight has fallen over my literary career. I've been writing a book all last winter and all summer. I just finished it before college reopened and sent it to a publisher. But yesterday morning the express parcel came and there it was, back again, with a letter from the publisher, a very nice, fatherly letter—but frank! He said he saw from the address that I was still at college and if I would accept some advice, he would suggest that I put all my energy into my lessons and wait until I've graduated before beginning to write.

And I thought I was making a notable addition to American literature. I was planning to surprise you by writing a great novel before I graduated.

I have already burnt the book.

I went to bed last night utterly dejected. I thought I was never going to amount to anything. But what do you think? I woke up this morning with a beautiful new plot in my head, and I've been going about all day planning my characters, just as happy as could be. No one can ever accuse me of being a pessimist.

Affectionately,
Judy

December 26

My dear, dear Daddy,

Haven't you any sense? Don't you know that you mustn't give seventeen Christmas presents?

Consider how embarrassing it would be if we should ever quarrel! I should have to engage a moving van to return your gifts.

Thank you, Daddy, a thousand times. I think you're the sweetest man that ever lived.

Judy

(Here's a four-leaf clover from Camp McBride to bring you luck in the New Year.)

January 9

Dear Daddy,

I address you, Daddy, from a bed of pain. For two days, I've been laid up with swollen tonsils. I can swallow hot milk and that is all.

"What were your parents thinking when they decided not to have those tonsils out when you were a baby?" the doctor wished to know.

I'm sure I haven't any idea, but I doubt they were thinking much about me.

Yours,

J.A.

(P.S. Where do you think my new novel is? In the wastepaper basket.)

March 5

Dear Mr. Trustee,

Tomorrow is the first Wednesday in the month—a weary day for the John Grier Home. How relieved they'll be when five o'clock comes, and you pat them on the head and take off! Did you ever pat me on the head, Daddy? I don't believe so—my memory seems to be concerned only with fat trustees.

Give the John Grier Home my love, please—I mean it. When I first came here to college, I was ashamed of the fact that I was from an orphanage. But now I don't feel that way in the least.

Give my kindest regards to Mrs. Lippett, the matron, and don't forget to tell her how well I have improved in the course of four years.

Affectionately,
Judy

Lock Willow,
April 4

Dear Daddy,

Sallie and I are spending a few days at the farm for the Easter holidays. We are having a fine time relaxing, reading, and writing.

What do you think is my latest activity, Daddy? You will think I am incorrigible—I am writing a book. I started it three weeks ago and this time I am writing about something I know; that is, life in the John Grier Home as an orphan.

Master Jervie and the editor were right; one must write about the things that one is most proficient in. I have a lot of hope for this book.

This new book is going to get finished—and published! You just see if it doesn't. I've learned that if you want a thing badly enough, and you keep on trying, you do get it in the end. I've been trying for four years to get a letter from you, and I haven't given up hope yet.

Goodbye, Daddy dear,
(I love to call you "Daddy dear.")

May 17

Dear Daddy-Long-Legs,

Commencement is going to take place three weeks from next Wednesday. I think that at least now you should come and show yourself to me. I shall hate you if you don't! Julia is inviting Master Jervie, since he is part of her family, and Sallie is inviting Jimmie McBride, since he is part of her family, but who is there for me to invite? Just you and Mrs. Lippett, and I don't want her. Please come.

Yours with love,
Judy

Lock Willow,
June 19

Dear Daddy-Long-Legs,

I'm EDUCATED! My diploma is in the bottom drawer with my two best dresses. Commencement was as usual, with a few showers at vital moments. Thank you for your rosebuds. They were lovely. Master Jervie and Master Jimmie both gave me roses too, but I carried yours in the class procession.

I am at the farm and think I'll stay here forever. The board is cheap, the surroundings quiet and conducive to a literary life. What more can a struggling author wish for? All I want is peace and quiet, and lots of time to work on my book.

Jerusha Abbott poses in her Commencement robes with Jimmie McBride and Mr. Jervie Pendleton

Master Jervie is coming up for a week or so in August, and Jimmie McBride is going to drop in sometime in the summer. He goes about the country, selling bonds. Jimmie will meet up with me during one of his travels.

I'd been expecting to have you come—only I know now that that wish is hopeless. When you wouldn't come even for my commencement, then I knew you wouldn't come at all.

Judy Abbott

P.S. The postman just arrived with a letter. Master Jervie will be arriving on Friday next to spend a week. That's a very pleasant prospect—only I am afraid my poor book will suffer. Master Jervie is very demanding.

Lock Willow,
September 19

Dear Daddy,

Something has happened and I need advice. I need it from you and from nobody else in the world. Wouldn't it be possible for me to see you? It's so much easier to talk than to write, and I'm afraid your secretary might open the letter.

Judy

P.S. I'm very unhappy.

Lock Willow,
October 3

Dear Daddy-Long-Legs,

I'm so glad to get a note written in your own hand. I am so sorry that you have been ill. If I had known, I wouldn't have bothered you with my problem.

Before I begin—here's a check for one thousand dollars. I've sold my story, Daddy. It's going to be published serially in seven parts, and then in a book. I owe you a great deal more than the mere money, and the rest I will continue to pay all my life in gratitude and affection.

Now, to my problem.

Master Jervie has asked me to marry him, and I refused. I love him, I really do, even though he is fourteen years older, but I was scared. And now he has gone away thinking that I refused him because I have feelings for Jimmie McBride—which is all wrong. I refused him, because I haven't told him everything about me; that I am an orphan and that I was raised in the John Grier Home. I was afraid he would not think it right for a person of my station to marry him, a truly rich and young Pendleton.

Maybe you've loved somebody too, Daddy dear, and you know how I feel?

Master Jervie is sick; he caught pneumonia while hunting in Canada. He is unhappy and so am I, but I love him.

Whatever should I do?

Judy

October 6

Dearest Daddy-Long-Legs,

Yes, certainly, I'll come to see you at your home in New York. I'll get ready right away, and I will find the way to your house. I am not a baby. You are awfully good, Daddy, to bother yourself with me when you are ill. Take care and don't catch a cold. These fall rains are very damp.

Affectionately,
Judy

Thursday morning

My Very Dearest Master Jervie Daddy-Long-Legs Pendleton Smith,

Yesterday, when I was escorted to your room and saw you, Master Jervie, when I was all the while thinking I would see Daddy-Long-Legs, I realized that it was a miracle. You were Daddy-Long-Legs all along. I should have known. There were so many signs all through these four years to make me realize it was so.

The doctor in your room said I must be a good nurse because in spite of your pneumonia, you are looking ten years younger.

Even if I turn ninety-nine years of age, I will never forget the tiniest detail of yesterday. The way your butler escorted me to your room. You getting up from the armchair, turning back to look at me, and then I knew—it was always you.

We belong to each other now, really and truly, no make-believe. Doesn't it seem queer, for me to belong to someone at last?

Yours forever and ever,

Judy

P.S. This is the first love letter I ever wrote. Isn't it funny that I know how?

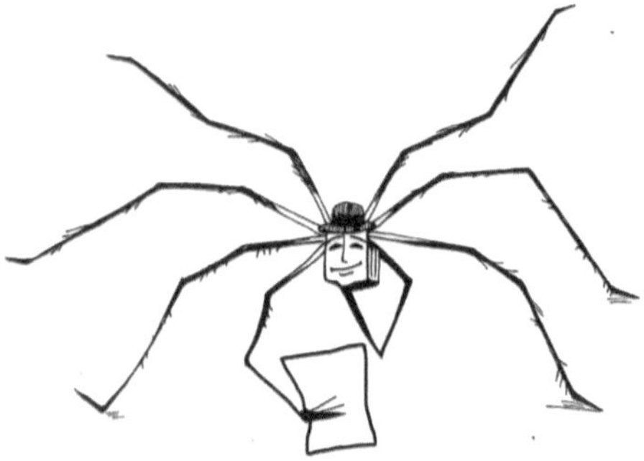

We belong to each other now, really and truly, no make-believe.

AVAILABLE TITLES

The Legend of Sleepy Hollow
by Washington Irving

Through the Looking-Glass
And What Alice Found There
by Lewis Carroll

Carmilla
By Joseph Sheridan Le Fanu

Daddy-Long-Legs
by Jean Webster

FORTHCOMING TITLES

The Canterville Ghost
by Oscar Wilde

Rip Van Winkle
by Washington Irving

Diary of a Nobody
by George and Weedon Grossmith

Agnes Grey
by Anne Bronte

The Picture of Dorian Gray
by Oscar Wilde

These titles, and many more, have been specially abridged by authors Fiza Pathan and Michaelangelo Zane for children aged seven to twelve. These books will introduce children to the rich repertory of rare classic literature which has not been abridged before now.

We invite you to subscribe to our email list so that you will know when new titles become available.

Email: fizapathan@fizapathanpublishing.com

Website: http://fizapathanpublishing.us/

www.ingramcontent.com/pod-product-compliance
Lightning Source LLC
Chambersburg PA
CBHW022200160726
48282CB00024B/262
9788193820193